Meet the WellieWishers™

The WellieWishers are a group of girls who each have the same big, bright wish: to be a good friend! Willa, Emerson, Camille, Kendall, and Ashlyn play together in a large and leafy garden cared for by Willa's Aunt Miranda. The girls all have garden boots known as wellingtons or "wellies." When they wear their wellies, the girls are ready for anything!

Are you ready to meet the WellieWishers?

Meet Willa

Willa is an explorer at heart, and with such a big garden to explore, she's always discovering something new! She especially loves climbing trees. From up high in the branches, she has a great view of Aunt Miranda's Garden. But no matter where Willa goes in the garden, she's always making new feathery and furry friends. Willa would do anything to help an animal. She helps the other WellieWishers enjoy nature, too.

Fun Fact:

Willa can speak Squirrel, Robin, and Rabbit—which comes in handy when she wants to chat with Carrot the bunny!

Meet Emerson

Presenting . . . Emerson! There's nothing Emerson loves more than being onstage. She sings, she dances, and she tells terrific jokes. Emerson is never shy about being silly—especially when she does it to cheer someone up. This talented performer is also great at getting her friends involved in her fun ideas!

Fun Fact:

This is Emerson's favorite joke:
How do you catch a squirrel?
Climb a tree and act like a nut!

Meet Camille

Splish-splash! Is that a fish? Nope—it's Camille! Camille loves swimming and pretending to be a mermaid. She also loves searching for garden fairies and making up her own songs. One time, she sang a lullaby to some sleeping butterflies! Camille loves her friends, too. That's why she's always willing to listen if they have a problem. She knows that being a good listener is one way to be a good friend.

Fun Fact:

Camille didn't always live near the other WellieWishers. She was sad to move away from her old house, but making friends with the other girls has helped her new neighborhood feel like home.

Meet Kendall

Kendall is full of ideas for making and fixing things. She takes a pencil and notebook everywhere she goes so she can sketch her latest idea. If she's got a tool in her hands, you can bet that a little while later—*bingo-bango!*—Kendall will have a new invention to share!

Kendall's crafts are also about being kind. She likes to make her own greeting cards from recycled paper and write sweet notes to her friends.

Fun Fact:

One time, Kendall helped her friends build a six-person seesaw!

Meet Ashlyn

Have you ever heard of Upside-Down Day, Walk-on-Your-Toes Day, or First-Day-of-Snow Day? Ashlyn invented them! She loves planning parties, so if there isn't a special occasion, Ashlyn makes one up. And Ashlyn always makes sure everyone is included in the fun, because every day is Friendship Day.

Stomp in Mud puddles

Fun Fact:

Ashlyn and the girls once planned a party to celebrate the day Carrot the bunny came to live with them. Hop, hop, hooray!

Explore the Garden!

The Playhouse

If you go to Aunt Miranda's Garden, you might find the WellieWishers in their playhouse. It's a cozy place to play pretend, sip hot cocoa, do crafts, make mud pies, or practice puppet shows. And with two walls that open up, sometimes it's hard to tell where the playhouse stops and the garden begins!

The Garden Theater Stage

The WellieWishers have put on many shows together at the Garden Theater Stage. They each contribute something special to the performance.

The WellieWishers have put on shows about rabbits, raindrops, and even rubber chickens! Things don't always go as planned. But the show must go on, and these five friends always find a way to make that happen.

The Tea Table

Some of the WellieWishers' sweetest moments happen at their tea table. It's the perfect spot to gather together! Whether they're celebrating a happy occasion or just taking time to talk, the WellieWishers make lots of special memories in this cozy corner of the garden.

Meet the Animals!

Carrot

The WellieWishers have a pet bunny named Carrot who lives in Aunt Miranda's Garden. Carrot's favorite thing to eat is—what else?—carrots! He also likes to be held and cuddled. Luckily the girls are always *hoppy* to give Carrot a hug.

Sir Chippington

This sneaky chipmunk lives in the big tree by the playhouse. He's always looking for something to eat and especially loves stealing bits of bread from the WellieWishers' sandwiches! The girls don't mind sharing, but they've learned to keep their food stashed in a cupboard.

Quackers

The WellieWishers met this duckling one day when he wandered away from his flock. They named him Quackers—his flapping and fluttering were so funny! But the WellieWishers realized that Quackers missed the other ducks at the big pond, so they took him home. Now the girls visit the pond every day to say hello to their feathered friend!

Norman

Norman the gopher is a bit of a troublemaker! One time, he took a mitten, a hat, and a bag of marshmallows from the playhouse. After searching high and low, the WellieWishers found their things in Norman's den. They weren't mad—they knew Norman was only trying to make his home cozy for the winter. But now the girls keep an eye on this goofy gopher!

Mrs. Honk

Mrs. Honk lives in the garden pond during the spring and summer months. When winter winds ruffle her feathers, she follows the flock to warmer places. The WellieWishers—especially Willa—are always sad to see her go. But Mrs. Honk returns to the garden every spring, and it's a happy day when she comes home!

A Year with the
WellieWishers

Rain, snow, leaves, or sun—there's no season the friends can't weather in their wellies! Here are some of the girls' favorite things to do throughout the year.

Winter

Let it snow, let it snow, let it snow! That's what WellieWishers wish for every winter. More snow means bigger snowmen, fancier snow forts, sledding, throwing snowballs, and more. When they get chilly, the girls warm up with tasty mugs of hot cocoa!

A little sparkle here, a little sparkle there . . . When Ashlyn is building a snowman, twinkle dust is just as important as a carrot nose.

A little creative thinking and some teamwork is all the WellieWishers need to finish a snow fort for their animal friends.

Spring

April showers bring May flowers . . . and lots of muddy puddles! Springtime is the perfect season for scavenger hunts, climbing trees, and getting wellies wet with rain. It's also the best time of the year to meet new animal friends!

The best part of mud puddles is splish-splashing through them!

Yellow—check! Red—check! The girls find as many colors as they can during their colorific scavenger hunt.

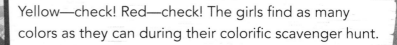

Tweet tweet! A new season means lots of new friends to meet, like this family of robins living in the tree near the playhouse.

Summer

Warm summer days mean icy lemonade, garden parties, and superhero games for the WellieWishers! Warm summer nights mean shimmery fireflies. What could be better than a twinkling light show at the tea table?

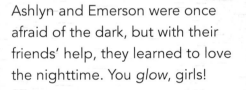

Ashlyn and Emerson were once afraid of the dark, but with their friends' help, they learned to love the nighttime. You *glow*, girls!

The Wicked Wellie of the West doesn't stand a chance against Glitter Girl, Agent Eagle Eyes, and Captain Quick!

Fall

In fall, the leaves on the garden trees change color and tumble down. But the WellieWishers aren't sad. They love seeing the garden change! Whether searching for fairies or throwing a fall fiesta, these friends always find ways to enjoy the season together.

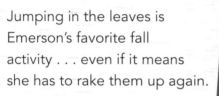

Jumping in the leaves is Emerson's favorite fall activity . . . even if it means she has to rake them up again.

But no worries! Kendall's super-handy *double-rake* can rake up leaves twice as fast as a normal one!

For Willa, Emerson, Kendall, Camille, and Ashlyn, every day in Aunt Miranda's Garden is an adventure in friendship. With wellies on their feet and love in their hearts, they know that being kind—rain or shine—is the key to making friendships bloom.

Turn the page to see the lyrics to the WellieWishers song!

The Welliewishers™
Theme Song

This is our WellieWisher song,
and when we've got our wellies on,
a little mud won't stop us
when it's time to play.
Splishing, splashing through it all,
Winter, summer, spring, or fall—
and we'll show you the WellieWisher way!

So put your wellies on your feet,
and start a-stompin' to the beat.
There's so many friends to meet
and things to do.
It doesn't matter who you are,
or if you're living near or far—
the WellieWishers wish the best for you!